Dear Parents:

Congratulations! Your child is taking the first steps on an exciting journey. The destination? Independent reading!

STEP INTO READING® will help your child get there. The program offers five steps to reading success. Each step includes fun stories and colorful art or photographs. In addition to original fiction and books with favorite characters, there are Step into Reading Non-Fiction Readers, Phonics Readers and Boxed Sets, Sticker Readers, and Comic Readers—a complete literacy program with something to interest every child.

Learning to Read, Step by Step!

Ready to Read   Preschool–Kindergarten
• big type and easy words • rhyme and rhythm • picture clues
For children who know the alphabet and are eager to begin reading.

Reading with Help   Preschool–Grade 1
• basic vocabulary • short sentences • simple stories
For children who recognize familiar words and sound out new words with help.

Reading on Your Own   Grades 1–3
• engaging characters • easy-to-follow plots • popular topics
For children who are ready to read on their own.

Reading Paragraphs   Grades 2–3
• challenging vocabulary • short paragraphs • exciting stories
For newly independent readers who read simple sentences with confidence.

Ready for Chapters   Grades 2–4
• chapters • longer paragraphs • full-color art
For children who want to take the plunge into chapter books but still like colorful pictures.

STEP INTO READING® is designed to give every child a successful reading experience. The grade levels are only guides; children will progress through the steps at their own speed, developing confidence in their reading.

Remember, a lifetime love of reading starts with a single step!

nickelodeon

TEENAGE MUTANT NINJA TURTLES

SPACE SHARK!

by Hollis James
illustrated by Patrick Spaziante

Based on the teleplay "The Outlaw Armaggon" by Gavin Hignight

Random House 🏠 New York

The Turtles and Fugitoid
are on a spaceship.
Leo is the pilot.

CHOMP!

The Turtles' ship is attacked by a space shark!

The space shark is
a bounty hunter.
He is hunting the Turtles!

Fugitoid thinks

the Turtles

should run away.

Too late.

Leo is already battling

the space shark!

Leo holds on tight
as the Turtles' ship
blasts off!

The Turtles land on
an old space station.
They will hide there.

The station's computer
comes to life.

It wants to destroy
the Turtles!

Mikey and Leo

bash the bots!

The Turtles are safe.

Oh no!

A giant SpiderBot

attacks the Turtles!

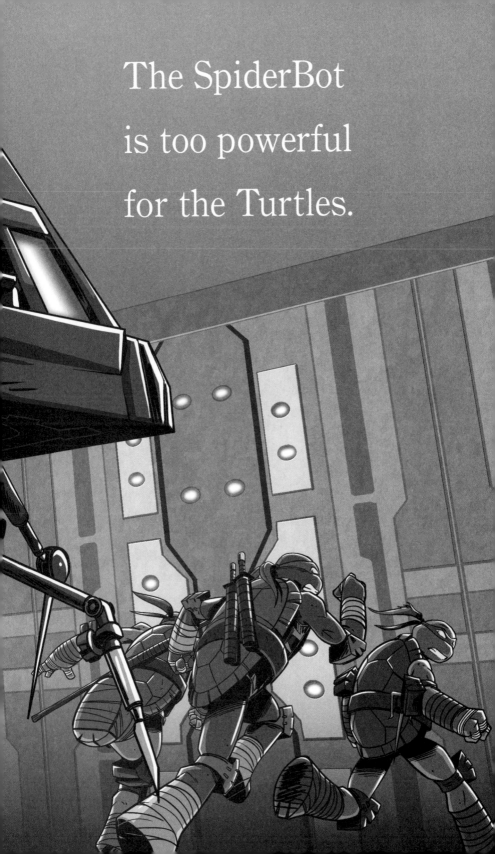

The SpiderBot
is too powerful
for the Turtles.

The space shark
stops the SpiderBot.
Why is he helping
the Turtles?

The space shark chases
the Turtles.

Run! Run! Run!

The space shark falls

through a hole

in the wall!

The Turtles zoom away
from the space station!

Booyakasha!

The Turtles are safe.